Rumi's Fables

Translated by

Negar Niazi, O.D.

Illuminated by Charles Colley, PH.D.
Edited by John G. Oster, M.D.

ISBN: 1480163023
ISBN 13: 9781480163027
Library of Congress Control Number: 2012920118
CreateSpace Independent Publishing Platform
North Charleston, South Carolina

"When you are with children, talk about toys,

From playthings, little by little, they reach

into deeper wisdom and clarity.

Children have a sense of wholeness in them already."

Rumi

✳ ✳ ✳

This book is dedicated to children of all ages.
May these stories remind them of the mysteries of life
and help them live a more joyous existence.

ᖰ᷈ Acknowlegments ᷙᖰ

I am very grateful to my soul teachers for giving me the opportunity to co-create this book with them. The journey of each story has been a soul healing and thanksgiving experience even in the face of a slowly debilitating disease like Multiple Sclerosis. At first the thanking for such a circumstance felt awkward, but with persistence it awakened my heart. In my gratitude, ten percent of the proceeds of this book will be donated to the National Multiple Sclerosis Society.

✲ ✲ ✲

"You have survived through many diseases because of the teachers you've known. Your limp has turned to a smooth step. Tie the cord around your ankle, so you don't forget what you've been given. Ingratitude and forgetfulness block further blessings they could give."

-Rumi

Rumi's Fables is a collection of Rumi's forty-three most magical and charming short stories that will entertain and educate the whole family. Rumi, the great poet and philosopher of the thirteenth century, has become, as talk show host Bill Moyers said on his television program, "the most popular poet in America." The United Nations called the year 2007 "the year of Rumi" to honor the 800th anniversary of his birth. Rumi's work has been translated into more than twenty-five languages and is being presented in a growing number of media, including workshops, music festivals, dance performances, and other creative outlets.

In this book, *Rumi's* Fables, over 25,000 lines from the *Masnavi*, Rumi's original Persian books, have been translated from Farsi into English. Although *Masnavi* is a book of devotional poetry, there are many whimsical stories thriving inside the poems. In this collection of short stories the author has hand-picked the most fascinating fables to entertain and challenge younger readers. *Rumi's Fables* comes alive with colorful characters — the sage king, the clever clown, and the bewitched prince — and many talking animals — the wise lion, the cunning fox, and the arrogant mouse. Each tale can be read as a simple bedtime story or as a profound and thought-provoking group discussion. At the end of each story there is a "contemplation box" to make the experience more interactive. There is also a summary of the moral of each story. These stories are reminiscent of the style of Aesop's fables. Readers, young or old, will find themselves in a land of mystery and myth that can transcend an ordinary or even a difficult life. These fables, with their deep and soulful content, communicate a personalized message to the reader.

About The Author

As an Iranian-American immigrant, Negar Niazi was brought up in a culture rich in ancient Persian literature and mythology like that of Rumi, Hafez, and Ferdowsi. Even though her educational background is in the sciences, with a B.S. in Chemistry from University of California Los Angeles and a Doctorate degree in Optometry from University of California Berkeley, her life challenges rekindled her passion for the works of Rumi and led her onto the path of a spiritual seeker. After Negar's life changing diagnosis of Multiple Sclerosis, she found herself on a journey into the world of mysticism, ancient literature, and mythology. She would like to share this new world through the magic of *Rumi's Fables*. Visit her website at *www. rumisfables.com*

About The Illuminator

Charles Colley became acquainted with *Rumi's Fables* as a talented painter and illustrator. After his initial reading of the first three fables, he fell in love with the stories. The tales became scenarios in his vivid imagination that he could hardly wait to bring to life through his paintings. He carefully studied each story and often dreamed about them at night, waking up enthusiastically to paint the fables. Every single illustration is an original hand painted acrylic on canvas. The paintings are works of love, imagination and creativity. A true artist at heart, he has indeed illuminated each fable. We will be forever thankful.

About The Editor

John Oster's involvement with *Rumi's Fables* originated from his knowledge of Aesop's Fables. After hearing Rumi's stories, he made the connection between the two. His interest in them has extended into a historical comparative analysis between these ancient works of art. His critical thinking and attention to detail have been of great value in the creation of this book. His encouragement and support have been a source of inspiration for this project. We are very much appreciative.

Table Of Contents

1. The Prince And The Village Girl

Thousands of years ago, there was a kingdom ruled by a handsome young prince. He was famous for his kindness and for the generosity of his fortune and spirit. One day the young prince decided to go hunting with a group of his friends. They rode on their horses to distant places, passing through many remote villages. As they were passing through one village, the prince saw a village girl whose beauty was unmatched. He fell in love with her instantly and invited her to his palace. The girl, overwhelmed by the majesty of the prince, agreed.

However, shortly thereafter, the girl fell terribly ill. The prince was heartbroken and called for the best medicine men from all over the kingdom. He promised big fortunes as the reward for the one who would cure his beloved. Each medicine man promised that he had the girl's cure. Each one claimed mastery of his craft but without any mention of the divine power. Even though each one tried very hard, they all failed terribly. Mysteriously, all their medicines produced the opposite effect of what they were designed to do. The girl continued to get worse.

When the prince saw this, he became very desperate and started to pray to God for a solution. He was in the middle of this intense praying when he fell asleep. In his sleep, he dreamed of a wise old sage who gave him this message: "The true healer will arrive tomorrow; he will have divine power and can do miracles." The prince woke up from the dream and the sun was shining so brightly that no stars were visible. He started to look out for the healer who was described to him in his dream. Medicine men kept arriving from all over the kingdom, but this time he knew who he was looking for. As soon as the prince saw him, he knew, for the healer was like a new moon, very bright but barely visible.

The healer was taken immediately to the girl's bedside. He started to examine the girl by first observing her pulse in response to a series of special questions. After a short while he came out of the room and told the prince he found the cause of her illness. He said, "Dear prince, the illness is caused by an emotional upheaval. During the pulse observation, I found out that there is a village boy that the girl is infatuated with, and the separation caused an emotional distress that triggered her illness. I know how to cure it; just follow my instructions."

According to the healer's instructions, the prince sent for this village boy. The boy and girl were allowed to be together once again. The girl improved rapidly and they lived happily together for six months. Then the village boy suddenly fell ill and the girl mysteriously lost interest in him, allowing the prince and the girl to live together happily ever after.

✶ ✶ ✶

Sometimes in life, good things (such as love) come with obstacles and difficulties. Be persistent.

> What would you do if you encountered a difficult situation?
> What if you tried everything in your physical power and still could not solve the problem?

2. The Farm Animals And The Lion

Once upon a time, there was a farm full of chubby and happy animals who lived together in harmony and peace. However, in the nearby mountains lived a fierce mountain lion who would come around regularly and disturb their peace by scaring them, and sometimes it would even capture one of the animals and take it back to its cave to feast on for dinner. One day all the animals circled around and planned a clever scheme to keep the lion from coming to their happy farm.

They all walked to the mountain where the lion lived and said, "Oh mighty lion, instead of working so hard to hunt us, we'll have a drawing amongst ourselves and send you an animal. This way you'll get what you want without having to travel to our farm, and in return, you have to promise to never step foot on our farm." The lion eagerly accepted.

After this agreement, everybody kept their end of the bargain for a while. Then one day at a drawing, the name of a clever little rabbit was drawn. The rabbit said to his fellow farm animals, "I have an even better plan that could set us free for the rest of our lives; all I need is some extra time." The animals got excited and accepted the small rabbit's idea. The rabbit took some time to purposefully make himself late for the appointed time with the lion.

Once he got to the lion's den, he found the lion very angry. The small rabbit said, "Oh mighty lion, I'm so sorry for being late. I was bringing you a fat and meaty rabbit, but we encountered a strange lion along the way and he stole the fat rabbit." The mountain lion got even angrier and ordered the small rabbit to take him at once to the place where the strange lion had been. The small rabbit obeyed the mountain lion and took him to a deep water well. He pointed to the well and said, "Look for yourself, it's in there."

As soon as the mountain lion looked in to the water well, he saw the reflection of a lion and at once jumped in the well to kill the lion that he thought had stolen his tasty dinner. As soon as he jumped in, he realized it was a trap, but it was already too late. The rabbit returned back to the farm and gave the news. The animals rejoiced and lived happily ever after in peace and harmony.

✻ ✻ ✻

The greatest physical strength cannot win over great cleverness.

How would you handle a situation if you were physically challenged
or not strong enough? Would you give up?

TAJ MAHAL
INDIA

3. The Secret Message From The Indian Parrot

traveling merchant had a beautiful parrot in a cage at home. One day he decided to take a trip to India to purchase more merchandise. Before leaving, he called together all of his family members, including the parrot, and asked them what they wanted as souvenirs from India. When it was the parrot's turn, the merchant asked him, "What would you like from India?"

The beautiful parrot said, "When you get to India and see parrots like me, tell them my life story and how I live in a cage in captivity, while they are free to fly anywhere they want." The merchant agreed. He reached India in one month's time on camelback.

When he finally arrived in India, he saw the same kind of parrots on tree branches. As he had promised, he told the story of his caged parrot to the free parrots. As soon as he told the story, one of the parrots on the tree fell to the ground, appearing dead. The merchant was very regretful about giving his parrot's message to the parrots of India.

When he went back to his village, he gave each person the souvenir they had requested. When he came to the parrot, the parrot asked, "Where is my souvenir?" The merchant said, "I'm very regretful that I passed on your message to the parrots in India, because as soon as I did, one of the parrots fell lifeless to the ground."

As soon as the caged parrot heard this story, it understood the secret message the Indian parrot had sent and he imitated it and fell to the bottom of its cage, appearing lifeless. The merchant was deeply saddened, and thinking the parrot was dead, he took it out from the cage and laid it under a tree to bury it later. As soon as the merchant turned his back, the parrot opened its wings and flew away.

✵ ✵ ✵

There is always a way out of difficulty. Be clever.
Seek advice from those who already know and have a different perspective.

When was the last time you thought outside the box to solve a problem?
Who do you go to for advice?

4. The Scholar And The Ship Captain

There was a scholar who was very arrogant about his knowledge and the numerous books he had read over the years. One day, he decided to set sail on a magnificent ship. He met the experienced ship captain and arrogantly asked him how many books he had read.

The ship captain, surprised at the question, replied, "I do not have any knowledge about scientific matters."

The scholar, in a demeaning attitude and tone of voice, said, "Then you've wasted half your life away by not learning the sciences." The ship captain was embarrassed by his mean words but did not say anything.

A few days later, when they were well into their journey and in the middle of the ocean, the sky became very dark and cloudy, and they found themselves in a huge storm. The waves were taller than the highest mountain they had ever seen. The ship was out of control now and in big trouble. In the midst of this commotion, the ship captain turned to the scholar and asked him, "Friend, are you familiar with the art of swimming in oceanic waters?"

The scholar replied, "I do not know how to swim even in shallow waters."

With candor and certainty, the captain told him, "Since you do not know how to swim, you have wasted *all* of your life, for this storm will sink this ship and there is no other way to stay alive than by swimming."

✤ ✤ ✤

Do not be arrogant in what you know, for there is always someone
who knows something that you don't.

What do you pride yourself on in life? Do you ever find yourself
acting arrogant because of it?

5. The Lion Tattoo

There was once a young man, known for his mighty strength, who wanted to get a tattoo of a lion on his shoulder. He went to a wise old tattoo artist. As soon as the tattoo artist put the tattoo needle next to the young man's skin, the young man yelled out in discomfort and asked the tattoo artist, "What are you tattooing on my skin? You are hurting me."

The tattoo artist replied, "Well, you asked me for a lion."

"What part of the lion are you starting with?" asked the young man.

"The tail of the lion," the tattoo artist responded.

The young man said, "Let's skip the tail; our lion doesn't need a tail."

The tattoo artist was bemused, but he agreed and put the needle on the young man's skin again. The young man screamed in pain again and asked the tattoo artist, "What part of the lion are you working on now?"

The tattoo artist replied, "The ear."

"I don't want a lion with ears," the young man said. "Let's make things easy and go to another part."

The tattoo artist agreed again, and again, as soon as he put the tattoo needle on, the young man cried and asked, "What part of the lion are you working on now?"

"The stomach," said the tattoo artist, starting to lose his patience by now.

The young man said, "The discomfort is too great, let's not do the stomach."

Finally the tattoo artist dropped all his tattooing instruments to the ground and said, "In this world has anyone ever seen a lion without a tail, ears or stomach? Even God himself has not created such a lion."

✲ ✲ ✲

If you want something in life, you have to bear the difficulties, taking the good with the bad. Nothing worthwhile in life ever comes without some form of hardship and struggle.

When was the last time you endured difficulty to achieve what you wanted?

6. The Lion, The Wolf, And The Fox

One day a magnificent lion teamed up with a fox and a wolf to go hunting for food. They were successful and captured a big wild cow, a mountain goat, and a small rabbit. The lion, who wanted to test the loyalty and wisdom of his two companions, ordered the wolf to divide up the prey amongst them. The wolf said, "Oh magnificent lion, you should get the big wild cow, I should get the mountain goat, and the fox should get the small rabbit." After hearing this, the lion got very angry, for if not because of his mighty power, there would have been no prey to speak of. In one swoop, he devoured the wolf, and then he turned to the fox and asked him to divide the prey.

After witnessing what had just happened, the clever fox said, "There is no need to divide up the prey, for the mighty lion should get them all, and should have the wild cow for breakfast, the mountain goat for lunch, and the rabbit for dinner." The lion, impressed by the fox's response, saw that the fox was generous and selfless. The mighty lion gave all the prey to the fox and said, "Because of your selflessness, we're one team, and the prey belongs to us, not to you or me."

✵ ✵ ✵

Teamwork and unity bring strength and abundance.
Learn from past events and do not repeat the same mistakes.

When was the last time you worked as a team and emphasized what was best for all?

7. The Snake Owner And The Thief

While a snake owner was taking his afternoon nap, a thief came and saw the snake and thought it was valuable. He stole the snake, but shortly thereafter, the snake killed the thief with a quick venomous bite. When the snake owner woke up and found his snake gone, he was very saddened and prayed hard to find it. As he was searching, he did not find the snake, but he found the lifeless body of the thief and saw the snake bites. He knew then that it must have been his snake that killed the thief. He had not known his snake was venomous and realized that the incident had saved his life.

✲ ✲ ✲

Sometimes when our prayers do not come true, it is better for us in the long run.

Were you surprised that the snake owner's prayers were not answered? Or were they?

8. The Donkey Owner
And The Tavern Keeper

A man riding his donkey reached a tavern in the middle of his long journey in the desert. He knew his donkey must be hungry, thirsty, and tired. So he decided to stop so they could both rest for the night. He asked the tavern keeper to give his donkey food, water and a place to rest. The tavern keeper got upset at this request and said, "This is my job, and I do not need you to tell me how to do my job."

The donkey owner, worried about his donkey, asked the tavern owner to soak the hay before feeding it to the donkey, for his donkey was old and his teeth were not sharp anymore. The tavern keeper replied, "I've been doing this for years, do not worry so much." The owner of the donkey went on, asking the tavern keeper to also put some medicine on the donkey's back, for he had some sore spots because of the long journey. Once again, the tavern keeper said, "I have had many customers and know what to do; as a matter of fact, I teach others how to take care of donkeys." The owner of the donkey was so tired that he finally went to sleep, trusting that the tavern keeper would keep his promise and take care of his donkey.

Meanwhile, the tavern keeper got busy talking to his friends and forgot all about the donkey. The next morning when the owner woke up and got ready to leave on his donkey, he found it tired and weak. It was then that he discovered that the tavern keeper had not kept his promise. From then on, he personally made sure that his donkey was well-fed and rested.

✵ ✵ ✵

Watch out for people who do not keep their promise.
If you want something done right, be prepared to do it yourself.

Which character in the story, the donkey owner or the tavern keeper,
can you relate to more? Why?

9. The King And His Eagle

There was a beautiful, high-flying eagle who was a frequent visitor to the king's palace. The king took perfect care of the eagle, as he was familiar with eagles. One day the eagle decided to fly away from the king. He flew away to distant territories, ending up at an old lady's cottage. The old lady, as nice as she was, did not know the first thing about caring for eagles. Thinking she was grooming the eagle, she cut the precious claws that the king had taken such good care of.

Meanwhile, the king went looking for the eagle. When he finally found the eagle, they were both immensely relieved, for the eagle realized that he was now with the person who knew best how to care for him, and the king was reunited with his beautiful eagle.

✼ ✼ ✼

Not everyone can see and appreciate the precious gifts bestowed upon them.
Do not take things for granted in life.

Who do you take for granted in your life?

10. The Prankster And The Townspeople

There was a young boy who had a bad habit of planting thorn-ridden bushes along the path of passersby. The thorns would rip people's clothing and get caught in their shoes. The townspeople kept asking him to stop, but he wouldn't listen. The townspeople finally took their complaint to the town judge and asked him to get involved. The town judge said to the boy, "You were told time and time again by the townspeople to stop planting these thorny weeds, but you did not listen. Now that the weeds have taken hold and their roots are much stronger, it will take you that much longer to clean up this mess than if you had stopped this bad habit when you were told. The longer you wait to clean up the bushes and get rid of this habit, the harder it will get, as the roots will get bigger and stronger, so do it soon before it gets completely out of control."

✻ ✻ ✻

Get rid of your bad habits as soon as possible, for the longer you wait, the more difficult it will be to get rid of them.

What bad habits do you have? What good habits do you have?

11. The Wise Man And The Sleeping Man

A wise man was riding his horse when he saw a poisonous snake approaching a man sleeping under an apple tree. Before the wise man had a chance to wake him, the snake bit the sleeping man. The wise man had to think of something really clever and fast in order to save the man's life. He rode his horse to the man, woke him up and made him eat all the rotten apples under the tree. The man, who did not know what was going on, begged the wise man to stop. But the wise man did not have time to explain, for the man could die at any moment. He made him eat more rotten apples until the man purged the snake poison along with the rotten apples.

✡ ✡ ✡

Sometimes in life, what seems bad is actually good and life-saving.

Can you think of a time when you thought you did not want to do something, but doing it was actually beneficial?

12. The Bear And His Friend

In the remote jungles, there was a bear that was always getting into trouble and making bad decisions that would put his life in danger. One day a strong man was riding his horse when he passed by the bear, which had been captured by a huge dragon, and was about to be eaten up. The courageous man jumped on the dragon and with his mighty strength freed up the bear. After this, the bear got very attached to the horseman and started to follow the man everywhere. Along the way, when the horseman got tired, they would stop for him to take a nap while the bear watched over him.

One day a wise man saw this and went up to the horseman. He woke him up to give him this advice: "You have befriended a bear who always gets into trouble; you need to stay away from such friends, for it won't have a good outcome for you." The horseman, who by now was used to the friendship, got mad at the wise man and said, "You're just jealous of this friendship. Go away; I won't take your advice." The wise man left, and the horseman fell sleep again. While he was sleeping, a few tiny flies landed on the sleeping man's face. The bear, trying to help, got a big rock and smashed the flies, but in the process hurt the horseman badly.

✡ ✡ ✡

Be careful about the friends you keep around, for their behaviors will eventually affect you even if they have the best of intentions.

What kind of friends do you tend to have around?

13. The Arrogant Mouse And The Humble Camel

A small mouse was walking in front of a big camel and was arrogantly pretending to be the leader. The camel who had noticed the mouse's arrogance did not say anything until they reached a deep lake. The mouse was now scared and stunned, not knowing how to cross the deep lake. The camel, seeing what was happening, thought it was a good time to teach the mouse a lesson. He said, "Dear mouse, why are you stopping? Lead on so that I can follow you."

The mouse said, "This lake is too big, and I am afraid of drowning."

The camel, playing along with his lesson, said, "Let me see how deep the water is." Then he put his long legs in to the water and said, "Oh it is not so bad, it only comes up to my knees. Why are you so afraid?"

The mouse said, "For you, it is not so deep, but for a small mouse like me, it would be too deep." Finally the mouse let down his arrogance and humbly asked the camel for help across the lake.

The camel saw that the mouse had learned his lesson and agreed, and they crossed the lake together.

✧ ✧ ✧

Do not be arrogant.
Even if the wise and strong may be humble, you should never
think of that as a sign of weakness or inferiority.

Do you know anyone who is both wise and humble?

25

14. The Boy With Three Bad Habits

A group of friends went to their village leader and complained about one boy who was bothering them because he had some bad habits. The leader asked, "What are those bad habits that are bothering you so much?"

They said, "He has three bad habits. One is, he talks too much. Two, he eats too much; and three, he sleeps too much. He does not know about limits."

The leader, after listening carefully, responded, "In order to be fair, one must understand that what is too much for one may be too little for another. For example, a puddle of water may be too much for an ant but is too small for a camel to be of any use. Even limits are relative. So it is not for you to judge him."

✾ ✾ ✾

Do not compare yourself with others. Some may look more or less smart or beautiful than you from the outside, but you do not know what is on the inside. So, do not judge.

How can you rid yourself of judgmental tendencies?

15. Four Different Ways Of Saying "Grape"

There were four friends who each spoke a different language. They could only partially understand each other. One day, they were given some money to buy food.

The Persian-speaking boy said, "Let's go buy some *angour* to eat."

"I want *estafil*, not *angour*," the Greek boy said.

"I know better," said the Manish-speaking boy, "let's buy some *uzum*."

The Arabic boy said, "All of you do not know, but the best thing to buy with this money is *anab*."

They were all arguing about this and the argument was starting to get really loud and turn into a fist fight, when finally a sage who could understand all four languages perfectly heard their argument and explained to them that they were all talking about the same thing. Once they understood this, they stopped fighting, bought some delicious grapes, and celebrated their unity.

✵ ✵ ✵

Most disagreements are based on a lack of true understanding and knowledge,
for there is only one truth.

When was the last time you were talking about something
and your friends completely misunderstood what you said?

16. The Baby Elephant And The Hungry Travelers

A caravan of travelers reached their destination in India. They were very hungry and wanted to go hunting for food. They came across a wise man who knew the area well; he said to them, "In this land, there are many herds of elephants. Be very careful not to hunt any baby elephants, for the mother elephants can smell their babies and will get vengeful." After this warning the wise man left, but after a while hunger took over and the travelers could not control themselves. When they came across a baby elephant; they got excited and hunted it for their dinner. Only one traveler was strong and wise enough to listen to the words of the sage; he was able to do the right thing in the face of hardship. He did not eat the baby elephant and stayed awake all night. The rest feasted and went to sleep. Just like the wise man had warned, the mother elephant came and smelled each person and killed all the travelers except the one who had not eaten any of the baby elephant.

✳ ✳ ✳

Nature is sacred and has to be respected and protected.
Listen to the words of the wise and experienced.
Doing the right thing sometimes comes with difficulty.

What would you have done if you were one of the hungry travelers?

17. The Pretentious Coyote

A pretentious coyote went to the house of peacocks because he wanted to look as impressive as one. So he put the colorful and soft peacock feathers that had been shed on himself. When he came out, he looked bright and colorful just like a peacock. He started to feel superior and wanted to show off to the other coyotes. He said to the other coyotes, "Look at how beautiful I am. I am a peacock from heaven." The other coyotes called his bluff by asking him, "Now that you are a peacock, can you sing like a peacock? Or does the whining sound of a coyote come out when you try to sing?"

✯ ✯ ✯

Watch out for those who show off and try to impress you by their appearance.
If you try to be boastful, eventually someone will call your bluff.
Do not pretend that you are someone other than who you are; the truth will eventually reveal itself.

Have you ever tried to impress others by pretending to be someone you are not?

18. The Snake Hunter And The Dragon

Early in the morning, a snake hunter went to the mountains to hunt for snakes. He searched for hours until finally he saw a tail sticking out of the snow. When he dug, he found a dragon buried deep in the snow. The dragon was frozen and seemed lifeless. With great effort he got the dragon out of the snowbank and dragged it back to his village. He planned to put on a show for the village people to show off the dragon and make money from it. People gathered from all over to see the body of the great creature. What nobody noticed was that as the sun was reaching its highest point in the sky, the dragon was slowly thawing out.

After a while, the dragon started to move his arms and legs, and the people got scared and started to run away in a panic. The snake owner, petrified, could not even move and was eaten up by the thawed dragon.

✵ ✵ ✵

Do not awaken the sleeping dragon. "Let sleeping dogs lie."

What do the above lessons mean to you?

19. An Elephant In A Dark Room

There are many elephants in India, but there are parts of the world that do not have any elephants. The Indians took an elephant to such a place and put it in a completely dark hall. Then they invited a few people who had never seen an elephant to go inside the dark room. Without any light in the room to be able to see, each person was asked to describe what they thought was in the room.

The person who touched the ear of the elephant thought it was a fan. The person who touched the leg thought it was a tree. The person who touched the back thought it was a cushiony bed, and the person touching the trunk thought it was a pole. After a while, they started to argue over who was right.

A wise man who knew what was going on, said, "If only they had the little light of a candle, they would know the truth and stop arguing."

✧ ✧ ✧

Keep in mind, everyone may think they have the answer, but it is only based on their personal experience. Try to understand other people's point of view and do not argue.

How can you apply this story to an argument you had with someone?

20. The Schoolchildren And Their Cruel Teacher

There was a cruel school teacher who was unfairly hard on her students. She would never give them a break and would give them so much homework that they would not have any play time. There was a clever student who said to her classmates, "I have a plan. If you all help, we can rid ourselves of this teacher for a while and take a break. Every time the teacher comes in the classroom, I will comment on how sickly she looks, and then each of you also make similar comments until she believes it and goes home."

The students followed this plan and finally, after hearing it so many times, the teacher believed them and went home to rest. The students finally got a few days off to relax and play.

✫ ✫ ✫

Be careful of words of praise or disapproval. Words can be powerful,

especially if enough people say them.

How do you react when people praise you or put you down?

21. The Eagle And The Stolen Shoe

A wise man decided to sit by the river to rest and meditate. While he was meditating, he took off the only pair of shoes he owned. Meanwhile, an eagle flew by and stole one of his shoes. While the eagle was flying, the shoe shook and a venomous snake fell out. Shortly thereafter, the eagle returned and flew by the river and dropped off the empty shoe by the wise man.

✴ ✴ ✴

Sometimes when something bad happens, it is for your own good.
Be patient when hard times come in life.

Can you remember a time when you lost something, but in time,
realized it was beneficial in some way?

22. The Language Of Animals

One day, a young man went to a sage who knew the language of animals and asked, "Can you teach me how to understand animals' language so I can better serve my community?"

The sage answered, "This kind of power and responsibility is not for everyone; you won't be able to handle it."

Day after day, the young man asked for the same thing and did not listen to the words of the sage. Finally, the young man said, "If you don't want to teach me the language of all the animals, then at least teach me the language of the rooster and the dog that I have at home."

The sage, after giving his final word of warning, granted the request. The young man, excited about his new ability, would stand in the yard every day and listen to the conversations between the rooster and the dog.

One evening after dinner, the leftover bread was put out in the yard. The rooster jumped and grabbed the piece of bread before the dog could get to it. The dog got angry, but the rooster said to him, "Don't worry, tomorrow the young man's horse will die and you can get a piece of that." When the young man overheard this, he took the horse to the bazaar and sold the horse, so he wouldn't take a financial loss.

The next day, the dog got angry at not seeing the horse and accused the rooster of lying to him. The rooster reassured him and said, "Do not worry, tomorrow the young man's donkey will die and you can have a piece of that instead." The young man, after hearing the rooster's words, took the donkey to the bazaar and sold it also.

The next day, when the dog saw that the donkey was gone, he got very angry and said to the rooster, "You are a big liar. Where are all your promises?"

The rooster said, "I promise you, I am not a liar, and tomorrow, the young man will get injured and there will be a big gathering with lots of food, and you can have the leftovers."

When the young man heard this, he got very upset and went to the sage to ask for help. The sage said, "I warned you that you would not be able to handle this kind of power and responsibility. The horse and the donkey would have provided you a means of escaping injury. By not listening to my advice, you have brought this misfortune upon yourself."

✤ ✤ ✤

Do not ask for things that you are not ready for. Not everyone should know everything.

When was the last time you insisted on something that ended up being harmful?

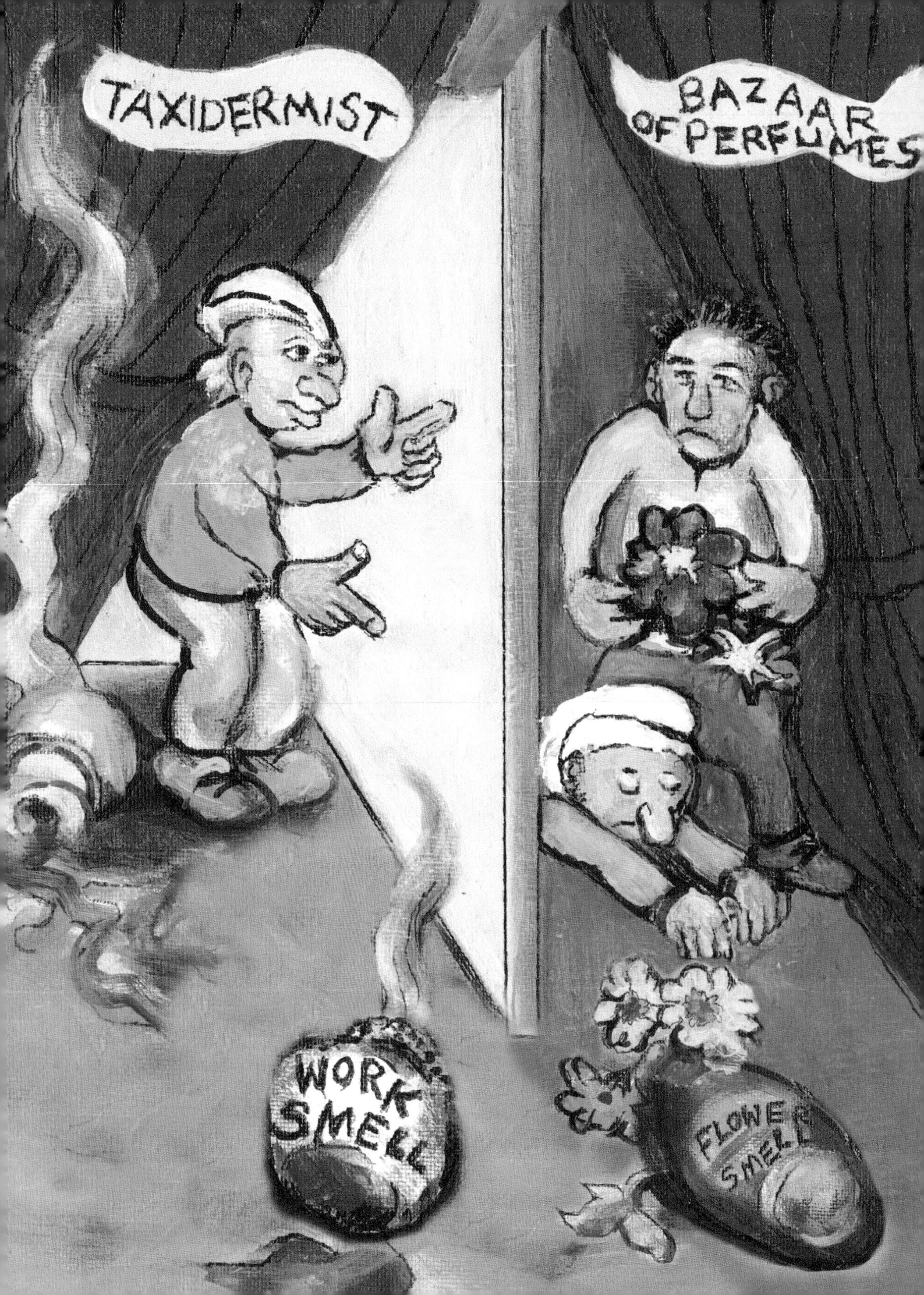
TAXIDERMIST
BAZAAR OF PERFUMES
WORK SMELL
FLOWER SMELL

23. The Taxidermist In The Bazaar Of Perfumes

A taxidermist, who liked his job, was accustomed to the smells in his workplace. One day he happened to be walking across a bazaar of perfumery. The whole bazaar was filled with the smell of flowers and herbal oils. The taxidermist, who was used to the malodorous smells of his workplace, got sick from the smell of flowers and passed out. Passersby gathered around, and not knowing what had caused this, tried to awaken him by splashing his face with rose water and other aromatics.

Unfortunately, none of these remedies worked. Finally, the man's brother came to the scene with a handful of ingredients from the taxidermist's workplace with smells that he was used to. He put them right under the taxidermist's nose. The people were stunned at what they saw. In a short time, the man gained consciousness, got up, and was his jolly old self again.

✲ ✲ ✲

Daily routines are habit-forming.
Do not assume what is good for one person is right for another.

What routines do you have that have become permanent habits?
Have you ever assumed to know what was right for someone else?

24. The Boy Who Liked To Eat Dirt

There was a boy who had a bad habit of eating dirt. One day he went to the village store to buy some sugar cubes. The store owner had a scale with weights made of dirt that he used to measure out his merchandise. As soon as the boy got a look at the weights made of dirt, he got excited, and when the store owner went in the back to bring out sugar cubes to be weighed, he furtively ate some of the dirt. The store owner noticed this, but he decided not to say anything and teach the boy a lesson. Since the boy had taken some of the weight off the scale by eating some of the dirt, he ended up getting fewer sugar cubes for his money.

✧ ✧ ✧

If someone cheats another person, he ends up cheating himself in the end.

What situation can you think of that cheating caused more harm than good?

25. The Poet And The King

A poet wanted to please the king and also make some money. He wrote a poem for the king. When he presented it, the king loved it and ordered his advisor to reward the poet generously with a hundred gold coins.

The advisor who was a very generous and pious man, agreed and said, "Oh generous king, surely such a poet deserves a thousand gold coins plus words of praise." The king was convinced and the poet was rewarded very generously.

The poet was very happy and wanted to know the source of all this generosity. When he found out that it was the advisor's counsel that had resulted in the king's generous reward, he wrote a poem for the advisor expressing his gratitude.

Years went by. The poet squandered his money and found himself in financial hardship, so he decided to write another poem for the king. He presented the poem to the king, who ordered the usual one hundred gold coins as his reward, but this time he had a new advisor. This man was very stingy and greedy. As soon as the new advisor heard about the reward, he went to the king and said, "King of kings, in light of the great expenses of the palace and the kingdom, we should not give a reward of a hundred gold coins; with your permission, I will talk him into accepting twenty-five gold coins."

The king said, "Do as you will." To add insult to injury, the advisor decided to make the poet wait for his reward.

Months passed by, until finally the poet's situation became so grim that he finally went to the advisor and said, "If you are not going to give me my reward, at least say so. All this waiting is making me sick."

The advisor saw this as an opportune time to offer the meager twenty-five gold coins, and the poet, who was very desperate by now, accepted the offer but was very disappointed. On his way out of the palace, he asked the gate keepers, "Why was I rewarded so generously the first time and so meagerly this time?"

The guards said, "Be thankful for this paltry amount, and leave the palace at once before the advisor changes his mind, for he is a very stingy and greedy person."

The surprised poet asked, "How is it that two people of the same position have such different characters and dispositions?"

✿ ✿ ✿

Just because people look the same from the outside and have some things in common does not mean they are the same on the inside or that they have the same values and characteristics.

When was the last time you formed expectations of someone
by his name or place in society?

26. The Boy And His Camel

There was a boy who wanted to go and visit his best friend who had moved a long ways away. He got on his camel and embarked on this journey, not knowing that the camel's best friend, the donkey, was going to be left behind. The camel did not want to go on this journey, for it would miss the donkey. Because of this, the boy and his camel were not a good match for this journey. Every time the boy would fall asleep along the way, the camel would backtrack, and the boy would have to go back and find it.

One year passed by and they were still in the middle of the desert, even though the trip should have only taken three months! The boy finally realized he would not get to his destination with this camel, so he got off the camel and set it free. Then the boy set off on foot for the rest of his journey, which went much more quickly this time.

✡ ✡ ✡

In order to get to your destination, all of the team members should have the same goal.

What would you do if you were working in a group and the members did not all have the same goal?

27. The Lying Traveler

A traveler who had just gotten back from a long and difficult journey was greeted by his friends. They were eager to hear all about his adventures. Even though he was hungry and his clothes were torn, he was very anxious, for he wanted to show off to his friends and make himself seem important. So he told his friends, "My journey was full of amazing adventures; as a matter of fact, I met a king who gave me many gifts and treasures and regarded me very highly."

His friends asked him, "If a king gave you so many precious gifts and treasures, why are your shoes and clothes all torn?"

The man responded, "Although the king gave me many precious gifts, I gave them all away to the needy."

His friends realized he was lying and said, "A person who gives away to the needy becomes peaceful and clearheaded, but you look and seem distressed and depressed. That's how we know you must be lying."

✾ ✾ ✾

A person's inner thoughts and emotions usually come out one way or another. Do not pretend to be something you are not. Clear your inside so it can shine through to your outside.

Have you ever been tempted to lie to impress people?
What happens if a person lies to impress others?

28. The Three Fish And The Fishermen

Three fish lived together in a river. One day, three fishermen who were passing by saw the fish and rushed to get their fishing poles. One of the fish, who was the most alert of the bunch, saw all the activity and became suspicious. She sensed the danger immediately and planned to leave the river and escape to the sea. The alert fish wanted to discuss this with the other two fish, but she knew they were stubborn and resistant to change and would only try to talk her out of it and ultimately slow her down. So she swam towards the open sea on her own.

The second fish, who was only half as alert as the first one, was startled by the sudden departure of the first fish. She realized there must be danger lurking nearby, so she planned an escape of her own. When the fishermen came, she pretended to be dead by going belly-up at the surface of the water. As soon as the fishermen saw this, they thought the fish was dead, so they placed her by the shore for later. The fish slowly flopped toward the open water until she was able to swim away to the sea.

But the third fish, who was not alert at all, was not aware of what was going on around her and had no plans of escape. She was captured by the fishermen and soon became their dinner.

�֍ �֍ �֍

There are three kinds of people. First are the people who are alert and lead the way. Second are the people who are not as alert but still have enough sense to follow the alert leaders.
Third are the people who know neither the right way nor how to follow.

Can you think of people who belong in each category? Which type of person are you?

29. The Bird With Three Pieces Of Advice

A man set out a trap and captured a bird. The clever bird said to the man, "In your lifetime you have captured many big animals like cows and sheep and feasted on their meat, and yet you are still hungry. What makes you think eating a small bird like me would satisfy your hunger for even a moment? However, if you set me free, I will give you three pieces of advice that will lead you to a lifetime of prosperity. I will give you the first piece of advice now, the second piece of advice when I fly to the roof of your house, and the third piece when I sit on the tree branch outside your house."

The man, intrigued by this proposition, agreed.

The bird gave his first bit of advice "Never look at the past with regret."

Then the man let him fly to the roof and the bird gave his second piece of advice: "Never accept an impossible proposition from anyone."

Then he flew to the tree branch and said "Oh foolish man, in my stomach I have hidden a precious pearl that weighs ten pounds. This pearl would have solved all of your financial troubles."

After the man heard this news, he got very angry and started to scream at the bird.

The bird said, "Did I not tell you in my first piece of advice to not regret things you did in the past? And with my second piece of advice, did I not tell you to not believe in the impossible? How could I possibly have a ten pound pearl in my stomach if I only weigh three pounds?"

Finally the man, who was very troubled by now, said "You have not told me the third bit of advice yet. Tell me the third piece of advice so at least I can learn something from this experience."

The clever bird responded, "Why should I waste my time and tell you the third bit of advice when you did not pay any attention to the first two?"

✻ ✻ ✻

There is no need for any further advice or regret if you are not willing to learn from past advice and experiences.

Which piece of advice do you like the best? Why?

30. The King And His Beloved Son

The king had a son whom he loved very much. The son was not only handsome but also very talented and smart. One night, the king had a dream that his son had an accident. When he woke up and realized it was just a dream, he felt relieved. But he decided to have a back-up plan just in case the dream was to come true. The king decided to marry off the prince so that the lineage would continue and he could have heirs to remember his son by. He started to look for a beautiful girl that his son could fall in love with. The king found a beautiful and pious girl, but the queen was very much opposed to this because the girl came from a poor family. However, the king insisted and the girl and his son were married anyways.

Meanwhile an old witch, who was infatuated with the prince, put a spell on him to make him leave his beautiful young bride. Shortly thereafter, the young prince left his beautiful wife for the old witch. The king was very distraught by this and sent for many medicine men to remove the spell, but they were unable to return the prince to his normal state. The king, who was desperate by now, started to pray.

In a short time, a wise man who was known for his extraordinary abilities came to the king. The king was very excited to see him and pleaded with the wise man, "My son has been changed under a witch's spell, please help us."

The wise man said "Do not worry; I have come here for this very reason. Just follow my directions closely and you can rescue your son from the spell."

The king followed the wise man's directions, and the witch's spell was removed. His son returned to his beautiful young wife, had many children, and they lived happily ever after.

✵ ✵ ✵

In this world there are many dangers and temptations, but with the help of the wise,
you can navigate safely through life.

Who has been a source of wisdom and guidance in your life?

31. The Clever Peacock With Missing Feathers

A beautiful peacock was plucking out his colorful feathers. When a passerby saw this, he thought to himself, "What a waste of beautiful feathers," and decided to say something to the peacock. He went to the peacock and said "How can you throw away such beautiful feathers? Do you know how valuable these colorful feathers are? You must be foolish and ungrateful."

The clever peacock responded, "Leave me alone, for you are a superficial person who only pays attention to outer appearances. These feathers I am plucking are the same feathers that hunters look for and put my life in danger. Tell me, which one is more important: saving my life, or saving my appearance?"

✡ ✡ ✡

Pay attention to what is really important in life and do not be misled by appearances.

What are your priorities, your appearance or your inner well-being? Do you ever find yourself looking too closely at appearances instead of other qualities?

32. The Deer And
The Farm Of Cows And Donkeys

A man found a deer while he was hiking. He captured it and brought it back to his farm of cows and donkeys. He put hay out for them and the animals started eating the hay vigorously. But the deer was agitated, jumping around and not eating at all. When the cows and donkeys saw this behavior, they started to ridicule and make fun of the deer. The deer stopped long enough to say to them, "Suit yourselves. Before I was brought here, I was grazing freely on fresh hay by the beautiful rivers and mountains."

One of the old donkeys, who had lived a long time at this farm, angrily protested, "Stop exaggerating and lying."

The deer said, "I am not lying, but because you are so used to captivity and being fed old hay, you cannot even imagine grazing freely on fresh greens by the river."

✵ ✵ ✵

When one is brought up in captivity (of the mind, soul, or body),
sometimes the person cannot even imagine freedom.

Do you know anyone living in captivity?

33. The Sultan's Humble Servant

Ayaz had been a loyal servant to a Sultan for a long time. Over time, he was promoted to a prestigious position in the Sultan's court. He was now a well-known and respected man, but he had a secret. He had saved his old uniform from the time when he was a servant in a back room to remind himself of his humble beginnings. To prevent others from finding out his secret, he put a big lock on the door of this room. His jealous colleagues, who had seen the big lock, were very curious about what was in that room. They became suspicious, thinking he was hiding gold and treasures stolen from the Sultan's court.

One day they went to the Sultan and explained what they had seen and tried very hard to convince the Sultan of Ayaz's betrayal. But the Sultan, who was assured of Ayaz's loyalty, decided to teach the jealous men a lesson. He said to the men, "Thank you for telling me this. Wait until he is not in that room and then go in and take all the gold and treasures and divide it amongst yourselves as a reward."

One night, thirty of the men eagerly broke the lock and entered the room. They looked up, down, left, and right and were dumbfounded when they did not find anything valuable, only the ragged servant clothing. They said to each other, "What are we going to say to the Sultan? What is he going to do with us?"

The Sultan, who knew the truth, said to them, "Why have you come back empty-handed? Are you hiding the treasure from me?"

The men bowed to the ground with embarrassment and asked for forgiveness.

The Sultan said, "I will not decide on your fate, since I was not the one who was accused. Ayaz should be the one who decides to either forgive you or punish you." He called Ayaz in and told him about the men and asked him to make the decision.

Ayaz, who had always been an obedient and loyal servant said to the Sultan, "Whatever I have is because of you and ultimately belongs to you. I will obey your will, whatever that might be."

✣ ✣ ✣

No matter where one is in life, one should stay humble and modest.

What was your last humbling experience?

34. The King Who Was Checkmated

One day, the king was playing chess with the clown who would regularly entertain him and his friends at the palace. In a very short time, the clown put the king in checkmate. When the king saw this, he got very angry and punished him. In order to redeem himself, the king invited the clown to one more game of chess. Even though the clown was scared this time, he agreed, and despite himself, he put the king in a losing position again. But this time the clown ran and hid behind the curtains before the king had realized what had happened. The king, who still had not realized he was in a losing position, asked the clown, "Hey, why have you left in the middle of the game? Where have you gone? What are you doing?"

The clown said from behind the curtain, "Dear king, you are in checkmate and have lost the game, and now I am ready for my punishment."

✲ ✲ ✲

Be careful of those who cannot accept defeat or criticism.

What happens to people who cannot bear to hear criticism?
What kind of people end up being their friends?

35. The King's Precious Diamond

One day the king gathered all his advisors and took a big precious diamond from his pocket. He gave it to the first advisor and asked him how much it was worth. The advisor said "More than a hundred pounds of gold."

The king said, "Okay…Now break it."

The advisor, who was shocked by this request and found it a waste to break such a precious diamond, did not do what the king ordered him to do. The king applauded him and awarded him with a gift. The king repeated this with four other advisors and they all responded the same way and were rewarded in the same way.

Then, it was the last advisor's turn. The king repeated his question to Ayaz, and Ayaz responded, "I cannot put a value on this diamond, but because it is your request for me to break it, I will obey." Then he got two pieces of rock and shattered the diamond into a million pieces. When the other advisors saw this, they got very angry at Ayaz. He replied, "There is more value in following the king's orders than in a diamond."

The king was very impressed by this and Ayaz became his most trusted and favorite advisor. Now the king wanted to punish the other advisors for their disobedience, but Ayaz intervened, and the king granted forgiveness to all of the advisors.

✫ ✫ ✫

*It is more important to follow the directions of the wise even in the
face of contradictions than to save material possessions.*

What might tempt you not to follow the wise? What would you do if someone
you trusted asked you to do something you did not want to do?

36. The Favorite Advisor

One day some of the king's advisors complained to him about his tendency to favor one of the advisors, named Ayaz, over all the rest. The king did not respond, but one day he invited all the advisors who had complained to him to go hunting with him. He saw a caravan at a far distance and asked the first advisor to go out and see where they were coming from. The advisor rushed out to the caravan and came back and said, "They are from the adjacent town."

The king asked, "Where are they going?"

The advisor got embarrassed because he did not have the foresight to get that answer. So the king ordered the second advisor to go out to the caravan. He came back with the answer and said, "They are going to Yemen."

The king then asked, "What merchandise are they carrying?"

The second advisor was dumbfounded, for he had not bothered to ask that question. So the king asked the third advisor to go and find out. The third advisor came back and said, "They are carrying pottery."

The king asked, "How much is it worth?"

Once again, since the third advisor had not asked, a forth advisor was sent out. This went on until all thirty advisors were sent out and the king had demonstrated their ineptitude. He then told them this story: "One day a caravan was in this area and I asked Ayaz to go out and see where they were coming from. When he came back, he not only had the answer to my question, but also the answers to the other questions I asked all thirty of you. Now, can you see why I favor him so much?"

✵ ✵ ✵

You do not need to wait to be asked to be a deep thinker; be thoughtful on your own.

When was the last time you went above and beyond the call of duty to accomplish a task?

37. The Ram Owner And The Thief

A shepherd owned a ram. He put a leash around the ram's neck so it would follow him. A thief who had his eyes on the ram found an opportune time and jumped out from behind a tree, cut the leash, and stole the ram. When the shepherd realized his ram was gone, he started frantically to look for it. As he was looking around, he saw a man sitting by a well who offered, "If you help me retrieve my bag of gold that has fallen into this well, I will give you one fifth of the gold coins. Since I had a hundred gold coins, I'll give you twenty gold coins as your reward."

The shepherd got greedy and thought to himself, "With twenty gold coins, I'll be able to buy not just one but ten rams." So he abandoned his search for the ram and rushed to take off his clothes and jump into the well. This was exactly what the thief wanted, and he stole the man's clothes as well and ran off.

✡ ✡ ✡

Be careful of greed and temptation.

Have you ever lost something in the promise of something more or better?

38. The Deceitful Tailor

A melodic storyteller was telling stories about a shady tailor to his audience. A man, who heard these stories got upset and went up to the storyteller and asked him, "Tell me, who is the shadiest tailor in your town?"

The storyteller responded, "There is a tailor named Pouresh who has no rival in stealing the clients' fabrics."

The man said, "I bet you he cannot steal even the smallest piece of my fabric."

The audience, who was amused by this proposition, tried to upset the man further by saying, "Many men more clever than you have been conned by this tailor. There is no way you'll be successful at this dare."

The man, who was very agitated by now, said, "I will take some fabric to this tailor and if he can steal even a small piece of the fabric, I will give you my valuable horse. But if he cannot con me, then all of you will be required to buy me another horse."

Everybody agreed, and the next morning, the man went to the tailor's shop with some precious fabric. As soon as he entered the shop, he was warmly greeted by the tailor, who asked the man very politely, "How can I be of service to you?"

"I would like a robe made of this fabric," the man said.

The tailor said, "Yes sir, it will be my pleasure to make you anything you like." He then measured the man for the size of the robe and went to work. As he was working, he was making small talk that the man found entertaining. The man started to enjoy the tailor's personality and stories. As the tailor took his scissor to make the first cut into the fabric, he told a very funny joke that got the man laughing so hard that he fell on the ground laughing. As soon as the man was on the ground, the tailor cut out a piece of the fabric for himself and hid it under his seat.

The man liked the story so much that he asked the tailor, "Please tell me another funny story."

The tailor continued telling funny stories and stealing more of the fabric. He was about to take a fourth piece of the fabric when he started to feel sorry for the man and said to him, "Do not ask me for more funny stories, or your robe will come out too small for you and you won't be able to wear it."

✵ ✵ ✵

Be careful of the amusements in life, for they can distract you from what is most important.

When was the last time you were distracted and missed what was truly meaningful?

39. The Poor Man And The Treasure

A poor man who was at the end of his rope kept praying for help, until one night he had a dream. In the dream, a wise man told him to go to a certain bookshop where he would find an ancient treasure map with instructions which would lead him to an immense treasure. When the poor man woke up, he excitedly went to the bookshop and found the treasure map with the instructions stating: "Go out of town to the broken tower, stand against the wall and place an arrow in a bow. Wherever the arrow lands, dig and treasure will be there."

The poor man bought a bow and arrow, went to the designated structure, pulled on the bow string as hard as he could, went to the landing site of the arrow, and dug out as much dirt as he could but did not find any treasure. Day after day, he kept doing this.

Meanwhile, the townspeople were starting to get suspicious. Afraid of being turned into the authorities, he went to the king and gave him the treasure map. The king, excited about the prospect of finding such an immense treasure, sent his best archer to do the task. The best archer shot arrows as hard as he could for months on end, until finally the king gave up and returned the treasure map to the poor man.

The poor man tried again many times without any success. He was very discouraged when he once again prayed for help. As he slept, he again saw the wise man from his dream who told him, "The instruction was to put the arrow in the bow and see where it fell. Nowhere in the instruction did it mention anything about pulling on the bow string as hard as you could. You did that on your own. Now go and follow the instruction and see where the arrow falls."

The poor man did just that. The arrow fell next to his foot and he dug the ground and found the treasure where he stood.

✫ ✫ ✫

The true treasures are closer to you than you think. Follow the instructions of the wise carefully and they will lead you to success.

Where do you think your treasure is hiding?

40. The Mouse And The Frog

A mouse and a frog were best friends. They would often enjoy spending time sitting together next to a river. One day the mouse said to the frog, "My dear friend, I would love to spend more time with you, but it is too bad that you spend a lot of your time in the water and I am only a terrestrial animal that cannot live in water."

The frog started to feel sorry for the mouse and at the mouse's insistence they came up with an idea. The idea was to tie a rope connecting their legs so that when one missed the other and wanted to see the other, one would just wiggle the rope and signal the other to come nearby.

One day, as the mouse was by himself near the river, a big raven flew by and took him in his beak. Since the mouse and frog's legs were tied together, the frog was pulled out of the water also and was dangling in midair. When people on the ground saw this they commented, "What a skillful raven to be able to catch a frog right out of the water."

The poor frog, who was helplessly suspended in midair, said, "This is what I get for having an unsuitable friend."

✣ ✣ ✣

Choose your friends carefully.

When was the last time you were affected by something your friends did?

41. The King And The Group Of Theives

One night a king disguised himself as an ordinary man and went walking around town. He came across a group of thieves who asked him, "Who are you to be walking at this time of the night in the empty streets by yourself?"

He responded, "I am just like you men. I am a thief looking to steal things."

One of the thieves, perhaps to test the new fellow, said to the rest of the group, "Men, let's reveal each of our talents."

The first thief said, "My talent is that I understand the language of dogs."

The second thief said, "If I see a person in the dark, I can recognize them in daylight, even if they are in disguise."

The third thief said, "I am the strongest digger you will ever see."

The fourth thief said, "If I smell the ground, I can tell if there is treasure hidden nearby."

The fifth thief said, "I am the best archer anywhere and I can capture the tallest castles using my bow and arrow."

Now it was the king's turn, and they asked him, "Now, tell us stranger, what your talent is?"

The king, who had been thinking about it, said, "All of my talent is in my beard. If there is a condemned criminal about to be executed, all I need to do is wiggle my beard and he will be set free."

When the group of thieves heard this, they were very impressed and said, "Indeed, you will be our leader, for in times of trouble, you are the one who can set us free." After this conversation, they all started to walk toward the king's castle looking to steal his gold and silver.

Along the way, they came across a barking dog. The thief whose talent was understanding dogs said, "Fellows, do you know what this dog just said? He said the king is among us."

However, the thieves were too busy thinking about finding gold and silver and did not pay any attention to the dog's message. Shortly thereafter, the thief whose talent was smelling the ground to find treasure, sniffed the ground and said, "There is no treasure nearby, just an old woman's cottage without a trace of anything valuable, so let's keep going."

They continued until they got to the very tall wall of the castle. The archer shot a rope using his bow and arrow, and they were all able to use the rope to climb the wall and get into the castle courtyard.

The ground smeller sniffed the ground and said, "This is the place where the king's treasure chest is hidden."

As soon as the excavator thief heard this, he started to dig. Everyone gathered around and collected as much gold and silver as they could and hid their shares at their homes.

The king, who was watching this very carefully, made sure he could recognize each of them later. The next morning, he sent his guards to their homes and had all of the thieves arrested. The thieves were immediately brought to the king's presence. At this time, the thief whose talent was recognizing people in disguise recognized the king and said, "O merciful king, now it is your chance to wiggle your beard and set us free."

✻ ✻ ✻

The best of talents is recognizing people for who they really are, despite all the appearances and pretenses.

Are you overtaken with appearances, or do you tend to look deeper? When was the last time you recognized the truth, even though it was not obvious? Do you think the king wiggled his beard and set them free?

42. The King And
The Maginificent Horse

One of the king's advisors had a magnificent horse that was not only beautiful but also powerful. One morning when all of the advisors were lined up on their horses in front of the king, the king saw the magnificent horse and was overtaken by its beauty and majesty. When he got back to his palace, he ordered his guards to confiscate the horse from its owner and bring the magnificent beast to him. The guards took the horse by force and brought it back to the king.

The advisor, who was very fond of his horse, could think of no other way to get his horse back but to appeal to the minister of the court, who was known for his kind and just nature. After hearing the advisor's complaint, the minster was very sympathetic and started to think of a plan that would get the horse back to its lawful owner. He went to the king and his advisors who were examining and praising the magnificent horse.

The king said, "Look at this graceful horse; isn't it perfect?"

The minster replied, "Yes, of course it is a beautiful horse, but if you examine it closely, you will see imperfections and asymmetries in his legs and body. Look at its head; it looks like the head of a cow." He continued such talk and said, "Indeed, now that you own this horse, it looks perfect to you, and you are willing to overlook all of the imperfections. You are looking at this horse with eyes that overlook all of the flaws."

Finally, the king began to believe the minster's words. He became discontented and ordered his guards to return the horse to its owner.

✳ ✳ ✳

Be careful of being influenced by other people's words.

What kind of language influences you the most? Can others
talk you into or out of certain situations?

43. The Man In Search Of Treasure

A young man inherited a huge sum of wealth but squandered it all away and was now living in poverty. One night, the hardship of poverty led him to pray deeply to ask for a solution. That night he dreamt of a wise man who told him to leave Baghdad at once and go to Egypt. There, his prayers would be answered.

By the time the man arrived in Egypt, he was completely out of provisions and money. After a while, not knowing what to do next, he decided his only option was to start panhandling. Since he did not look like a poor person and was embarrassed to beg, he decided to wait until nighttime to panhandle, so people would not recognize him.

As it happened, the city was on high alert to look out for robbers and thieves at nighttime. At nightfall the man was wandering the streets still deciding if he should start panhandling, when the city guards saw him and arrested him. One of the guards asked him, "What are you doing in the streets at night? Where is the rest of your gang of thieves? Which house are you going to rob next?" The man begged the guard to stop and listen to his story. The guard could tell the man was not a thief and was telling the truth by the way he was talking.

After listening to the whole story, the guard thought the man was naive to come all the way to Egypt because of a dream of treasure. With pity and a bit of sarcasm, the guard said to the man, "Friend, you have taken such a long and hard journey to Egypt just because of a dream of treasure! Are you a fool? Many times I also have had dreams of a treasure hidden in Baghdad in a certain town, in a certain street, in a certain house. But I have never taken it so seriously as to leave Egypt and make a hard journey in pursuit of it. Look at how stupid you have been."

The man, after hearing the guard's dream about Baghdad and the directions to where the treasure lay, realized that the guard's dream had the precise directions back to his own house in Baghdad. He realized the message was that the treasure was actually hidden under his own house all along. He also realized that he had to go through the hardship of the journey in order to discover the treasure.

✻ ✻ ✻

Even though the true treasure in life is usually closer than you think,
it often takes some hardship to find it.

What hardship have you endured to get you closer to the true treasure in life?
What does the true treasure in life mean to you?

REFERENCES

The translations and commentaries of the great Rumi scholars, Karim Zamani and Reynold A.Nicholson were cross-referenced to reinsure accuracy.

The *Masnavi* references for each fable are listed below, with the Roman numerals for the volume, I-VI, followed by line numbers.

1. THE PRINCE AND THE VILLAGE GIRL- I;35-246
2. THE FARM ANIMALS AND THE LION- I   ;900-1201
3. THE SECRET MESSAGE FROM THE INDIAN PARROT- I;1547-1907
4. THE SCHOLAR AND THE SHIP CAPTAIN- I;2835-2980
5. THE LION TATTOO- I;2981-3012
6. THE LION, THE WOLF, AND THE FOX- I;3013-3055
7. THE SNAKE OWNER AND THE THIEF- II;135-155
8. THE DONKEY OWNER AND THE TAVERN KEEPER- II;156-313
9. THE KING AND HIS EAGLE- II;323-375
10. THE PRANKSTER AND THE TOWNSPEOPLE- II;1227-1245
11. THE WISE MAN AND THE SLEEPING MAN- II;1878-1931
12. THE BEAR AND HIS FRIEND- II;1932-2094
13. THE ARROGANT MOUSE AND THE HUMBLE CAMEL- II;3436-3477
14. THE BOY WITH THREE BAD HABITS- II;3506-3640
15. FOUR DIFFERENT WAYS OF SAYING "GRAPE"- II;3681-3712
16. THE BABY ELEPHANT AND THE HUNGRY TRAVELER- III;69-235
17. THE PRETENTIOUS COYOTE- III;721-839
18. THE SNAKE HUNTER AND THE DRAGON- III;976-1156
19. AN ELEPHANT IN A DARK ROOM- III;1259-1385
20. THE SCHOOLCHILDREN AND THEIR CRUEL TEACHER- III;1522-1613
21. THE EAGLE AND THE STOLEN SHOE- III;3238-3265
22. LANGUAGE OF ANIMALS- III;3266-3516
23. THE TAXIDERMIST IN THE BAZAAR OF PERFUMES- IV;257-352
24. THE BOY WHO LIKED TO EAT DIRT- IV;625-725
25. THE POET AND THE KING- IV;1156-1357
26. THE BOY AND HIS CAMEL- IV;1533-1577
27. THE LYING TRAVELER- IV;1739-1801
28. THE THREE FISH AND THE FISHERMEN- IV;2202-2242
29. THE BIRD WITH THREE PIECES OF ADVICE- IV;2245-2508
30. THE KING AND HIS BELOVED SON- IV;3085-3241
31. THE CLEVER PEACOCK WITH MISSING FEATHERS- V;536-832
32. THE DEER AND THE FARM OF COWS AND DONKEYS- V;833-844
33. THE SULTAN'S HUMBLE SERVANT-V;1857-1999
34. THE KING WHO WAS CHECKMATED-V;3507-3534
35. THE KING'S PRECIOUS DIAMOND- V;4035-4238
36. THE FAVORITE ADVISOR - VI;385-434

Made in the USA
Charleston, SC
07 February 2013